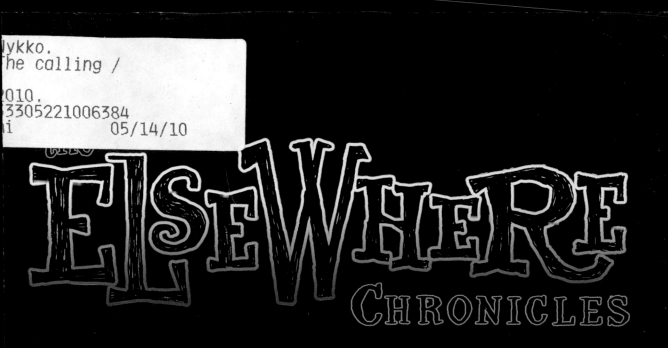

ELSEWHERE
CHRONICLES

BOOK FOUR
THE CALLING

ART
BANNISTER

STORY
NYKKO

COLORS
JAFFRÉ

GRAPHIC UNIVERSE™ · MINNEAPOLIS · NEW YORK

A huge thank you to Flo for his
indispensable daily support
Bravo to Laurence, Nykko, Corentin, and Mathilde
for having the courage to leap into a second cycle
Thank you to Denis and to everyone who
worked on this series both near and far
—Bannister

To my two adventurers, Léo & Noé
To Sabine, my Warrior Princess
To Andrée—may Ilmahil light her path
—Nykko

To Mathilde and my Parents
—Jaffré

3

Well, now you two don't look any better than I do.

I think, today, that the doctors are wrong. They don't really know what I have, because it comes from the other side of the mirror. The other world. Elsewhere.

It was a ghost who led me to you. Whenever he's near me, he reassures me and I feel in great shape, like before.

When I don't see him, I get weak and start hurting again.

Tell us this is a really unfunny joke, Rebecca!

You don't look well, Rebecca. You should go see a doctor.

JUNK

No, I told you. They can't do anything for me!

The ghost will return, and I will get better. You guys will see.

You don't believe me?

But how will I find a passageway? Everything was destroyed.

While the great scriptwriter was creating his craziness, I had time to read Grandpa Gabe's books.

I remember very clearly reading that it's possible to open a passageway with the machine, provided you follow a few rules precisely.

Here it is!

Hey, my figures!

It's all written in here. What it does, is it finds an access point.

A mirror, a wall of ice, some naturally polished quartz, even a frozen lake!

You were better off in my room.

Right there! That should be enough to duplicate the pattern exactly.

Noah, you get the mirror!

We're going to find this passageway!

All right, but fast, okay?

SHLAK

Rebecca, you must turn it as delicately as possible.

FLASH

Go ahead, Noah. Start moving the mirror.

I think I know what to do. This reminds me of the time when my dad spent two days trying to set up a satellite dish to pick up some TV channels.

If he's anything like mine, he ended up calling a professional after getting all worked up about how the equipment supposedly wasn't made right.

Pretty much. But, it's a well-known fact, kids are often more gifted than their parents. Hehe . . .

I'm going to jam the machine's countdown mechanism. That'll keep me from having to turn it back on every two minutes.

Do you think that's wise?

As long as we stay on this side of the mirror, we're not taking many risks.

There.

29

33

Don't make that face, kid! I was bringing in my dinner when I surprised you.

If you want the right to eat, you have to help me. Our little altercation exhausted me.

Bruiser...

And I want to know all about your friends. The fact that you have discovered my secret... worries me.

For sure it was that homeless guy Bruiser who was buried in your place.

The police thought Bruiser had kidnapped us, because nobody could find him. As far as they know, he's hiding out, when in reality, he's dead and buried.

The Perryville police were never very bright.

But then, that means you killed Bruiser to set up your fake funeral!

Aren't you a clever boy!

That pilfering scoundrel took up a bad habit of squatting in my house and wearing my clothes when I was away. He got too curious and opened the passageway.

I was negligent.

I suppose the shock was too much for him. When I found him, he had been dead for many days.

A heart attack, no doubt.

I'm sorry, I know this is all my fault, but please... make up!

I already apologized. Yes, I made a little mistake. But I'm suffering as much as you are in all this.

No kidding!

We're in the middle of nowhere and maybe stuck here for life because little Mister Theo made a little mistake! Because of you, my parents are gonna get divorced!

You're really gullible to think you can stop them.

I'll show you who's gullible! Take off your glasses!

Noah, stop! It's me you should be blaming.

No, Rebecca. Noah's right! I'm the only one to blame, and I'm going to take responsibility for it.

And, in the end, at least I have the satisfaction of knowing you're almost healed.

45

To be continued...

Art by Bannister
Story by Nykko
Colors by Jaffré
Translation by Carol Klio Burrell

First American edition published in 2010 by Graphic Universe™.
Published by arrangement with Mediatoon Licensing—France.

Copyright © by Dupuis 2009—Bannister, Nykko
English translation copyright © 2010 Lerner Publishing Group, Inc.

Graphic Universe™ is a trademark of Lerner Publishing Group, Inc.

Graphic Universe™
A division of Lerner Publishing Group, Inc.
241 First Avenue North
Minneapolis, MN 55401 U.S.A.

Website address: www.lernerbooks.com

Library of Congress Cataloging-in-Publication Data

Bannister.
Book four: The calling / art by Bannister ;
story by Nykko. — 1st American ed.
p.   cm. — (ElseWhere chronicles ; bk. 4)
Summary: Rebecca, convinced that she will die if she does not
return to the other world, enlists the help of Theo and Noah to open
a new passageway, but once on the other side they fall into danger
and Max, unaware of the peril, follows.
ISBN: 978-0-7613-6068-1 (lib. bdg. : alk. paper)
1. Graphic novels. [1. Graphic novels. 2. Horror stories.] I. Nykko.
II. Title.
PZ7.7.B34Cal 2010
741.5'973—dc22   2009037643

Manufactured in the United States of America
1 – BP – 12/15/2009